THE LOST UNIVERSE

THE LOST UNIVERSE

ALDIVAN TORRES

Canary Of Joy

CONTENTS

1   1

CHAPTER 1

The Lost Universe
Aldivan Torres
The Lost Universe

Author: Aldivan Torres
© 2020- Aldivan Torres
All rights reserved.

This book, including all its parts, is protected by Copyright and cannot be reproduced without author's permission, or transferred.

Aldivan Torres, born in Brazil, is a consolidated writer in various genres. So far, the titles have been published in dozens of languages. Since his age, he's always been a lover of the art of writing, having consolidated a professional career from the second semester of 2013. Your mission is to conquer the heart of each of your readers. In addition to literature, its main amusements are music, travels, friends, family, and the pleasure of life itself. "For literature, equality, fraternity, justice, dignity, and honor of human being always" is your motto.

Book Content
The Lost Universe 1
The Lost Universe 2
The Lost Universe 3
The Lost Universe 4

The Lost Universe 5
The Lost Universe 6
The Lost Universe 7

The Lost Universe 1

Camping in the woods

Cabin at night

Divine

I am pleased to be with you again. All this atmosphere magic of the mountain inspires me a dream with stories mysterious. In my mind, they are stories without direction that I need to drive, and you are part of it.

Renato

It is a great pleasure to participate in all of this, my beloved seer. We were looking forward to you because the series "The Seer" needs to continue. I'm confident that our followers were eager for this meeting.

Guardian

You are right. The time has come for our challenge. I feel exciting challenges in front of us. We urgently need to act to save worlds and transform lives. We are the team of the most important saga in the world. Furthermore, we need takes on this responsibility.

Divine

I know that, master. That's what guided me up here. I'm aware of my duties together with our fans. I will not disappoint them. Here begins a new story. What you say to that, spirit of the mountain?

Guardian

There is a parallel world in destruction. Terrifying beings have invaded this world and want to dominate it. There is a cry for mercy. I feel like this is our chance to help. We can neutralize these threats with our mind.

Divine

Interesting. What a monstrous danger! The universe and its secrets. Despite the knowledge I have, this surprise me. What if we fail? What happens to us?

Guardian

We will believe in our ability. "The Lost universe " is a world peaceful and need of our help. What would you do if your friends were in danger? We need to analyze what is important at this point.

Divine

You're right. I would save my friends. A true friend is one who gives his life for the other. I am the faithful and legendary son of David. Nothing scares me. We will face the dangers with divine strength. I am convinced that God is on our side.

Renato

I also have this confidence. Let's face the danger together. We are ready for anything.

Guardian

I liked your willpower. Now, how about some dinner? I will prepare a wonderful soup for you.

Divine

I am a person who follows a natural diet and healthy practices. Furthermore, I will love the soup. I love the foods typical to the Northeast.

Renato

I also like the food natural. In fact, I think I like to eat everything. The poor have no choice. We have to eat what is available.

Guardian

Very well, my loves. Let's go into the cabin.

Kitchen

After the dinner

Divine

The soup was delicious. Thanks for the welcome. I don't know how to thank you.

Guardian

How did you spend this time when we were apart? I am quite curious.

Renato

I am also very curious. Could you tell us, my friend?

Divine

Of course, yes. I spent very well. I remain engaged in my professional and artistic projects. In the field of literature, I will publish books in Portugal, Brazil and India. In the field of cinema, I already have eight completed films. In the field of music, I am always composing beautiful songs. I will never give up on my dreams.

Guardian

I admire your disposition, and I am at your side. Dreams were meant to be realized. In, However, the majority of people give up before the first difficulty. This is not your case. You climbed the mountain, faced challenges, entered the cave more dangerous in the world and won. I am proud of your ability and your faith.

Divine

Thank you. Without the help of you, I wouldn't be able to so much progress.

Renato

I am happy with your recognition. Together, we are stronger.

Divine

I know how to be grateful. Sorry, but now I'm going to sleep. Good night to all.

Renato

Sleep in peace.

Guardian

Great night.

Divine Room

Angel

Don't go to sleep yet, Divine. I need to talk to you.

Divine

You can talk, angel.

Angel

An adventure is about to begin. You will get to know "The Lost Universe ", a world totally desperate in the face of chaos. Do you have any idea what that would mean?

Divine

I am aware that the danger is very great. I feel that there is a great chance of failure. But what can I do? I love the beings created by my father. I'm not leaving any of them.

Angel

Excellent. Congratulations on your courage. I am with you. Let's face this challenge together.

Divine

You're going with me?

Angel

I will always be with you, but invisibly. I'm your angel, remember?

Divine

I remember. Thanks for the support.

Angel

You're welcome! Always count on me. Good night.

Portal

guardian

This is the entry for "The Lost Universe". The advice I can give is caution and patience at all times. We will believe in divine protection.

Renato

I'm with fear, but this is what I've always dreamed of. Let's move on.

Divine

Don't worry about anything. We will face the situation and try to save this world. It is our obligation. We are ready!

Field (between the trees)

Divine

My God. We have been walking for so long and no sign of civilization. We're lost?

Guardian

My dear, "The lost universe" is a gigantic world. What is happening is absolutely normal.

Renato
Can we stop a second? I'm tired.
Guardian
All right. As long as it is for a short time.
Renato
Take advantage and teach us something, son of God.
Divine
Well thought out, Renato. Being here is one great opportunity to contemplate the nature. We need to connect to this force natural called " Mother Earth". This brings us several benefits.
Renato
I understand your point of view. Currently, being human forgotten their origins and focuses on materialism. We've lost a good and important part of our humanity.
Guardian
We need to have an analysis of global awareness of ethical concepts and values. Furthermore, we need to reinforce the honesty and our simplicity. Only then can we finally evolve.
Divine
I emphasize the charity, the integrity and honor. But we are free. Let's move on?
Guardian
Come on! I think about that.
Another field
Guardian
the attacks began
Divine
oh my god!
Renato
oh my god!

The Lost Universe 2

In the indigenous village

Shaman

Welcome strangers. We were waiting for you.

Guardian

Thank you. I am the spirit of the mountain, the guardian of the most hidden secrets. We came to your world because we felt a cry for help. Despite the danger, we came to help. We do not abandon those in need. Who are you?

Shaman

I am the shaman of the northern tribe. My people and I are resisting the invasion of the monsters. Thanks to my astral knowledge, good spirits protect us. But we are helpless because we have not been able to expel the invaders. That's why I called you here telepathically. I know your trajectory. You are the most successful adventurers in the world.

Guardian

You made the right decision. It is an honor to be able to contribute to the peace of this world. We are committed to good causes. We have power, talent, and intelligence. This is what defines our team.

Shaman

Very well. Introduce yourself, guys. You make yourself comfortable.

Divine

My name is Divine. But you can call me a psychic or a child of God. I am the protagonist of this story. I am very grateful for this opportunity. You can count on me for anything. I love exciting and challenging adventures.

Shaman

That's great, Divine. I admire hard-working young people. I always dreamed of this day. Meeting the son of God makes me pleased.

Divine

I am also thrilled with this meeting.

Renato

My name is Renato. We have come a long way to try to free you. We are specialists in recovering destroyed worlds. In the adventures of our saga, we travel in time, control "the darkest night of our souls", go back to the past and discover secrets, unveil "The God's code", reaffirm our values and cry out for freedom in book "I am", we travel through space and face demons, we discover the concept of Wicca witchcraft, and we learn to respect religions. Anyway, the list is exhaustive. We are always active in transforming the world into a better place.

Shaman

Amazing! I have no doubt that I am before the most evolved beings in the universe. You are our hope. We need to believe that we will survive this plague. We want to get back in touch with "Mother Earth" and cultivate our spirituality. Everyone should enjoy what life has to offer. But come in. We need to talk more.

Renato

Thanks for the invitation. Let's go, guys?

Divine

Of course. It will be an honor.

Guardian

We were waiting for the invitation.

Interior of the house- village

Shaman

Divine, my friend, your life has not been easy. Am I right?

Divine

Truth. Since I was born, I face great difficulties. My life has been a great battle. I was born in northeastern Brazil, amid great social inequalities. I faced misery, indifference, and rejection. They were troubled and challenging moments. Nobody has ever encouraged me in my activities. I had to live day after day, conquering little things. Today, I am a composer, writer, filmmaker and civil servant. There is still a long way to go, but my dreams remain with me. I aim to win the Nobel Prize for literature and Oscar. I know it's a difficult task, but it is not impossible for God. It is my faith that sustains me and leads me to accomplishments. I still believe in my success, although it may take a while.

Shaman

It's a beautiful testimonial. You have the spirit of the great warrior. I didn't have an easy life, either. In my childhood, nobody believed in me because I belonged to a lower lineage. I had to go through countless tests until I became the tribe's shaman. I know how you must feel. It is as if we are swimming against a strong current in the river and cannot move forward. Faith is a greater force than the current. Believe in your dreams, young man.

Divine

I will always believe. Storytelling is truly motivating for me.

Shaman

We have a beautiful group. Congratulations, mountain spirit. His training had an effect. We have two young people here capable of changing the destiny of the world. Not only with actions, but also as an example of life. What does the world expect of us? I answer. We need spiritual guides. Someone capable of facing dangers without hesitation. Only then the universe will have peace.

Guardian

It is their merit. I was just an instrument of destiny. I am proud of the evolution of my disciples. They have certainly surpassed me in wisdom and power. But we stay together because we need each other.

Renato

Truth. I will always need you, my mother. I will never forget its strategic importance in my life. You two complete me. Before meeting them, I lived a miserable life with my father. My release brought me new perspectives on life. Finally, I can hope that I will be happy.

Weeping Guardian

It moves me, son. Knowing that I am dear is significant to me. I will always support you. You deserve the best in life. I have a responsibility to promote the good in the universe.

Divine

I know how you suffered, Renato. Thankfully, this was just a phase. We are together now in this new adventure. We promise to act to free your people, dear shaman.

Shaman

I appreciate your goodwill. I made the right choice. There will be many challenges to face, but be prudent and courageous. My spirit will be with you.

Divine

Thank you. We have to go. A new challenge is presented.

Shaman

Good luck to everyone.

The Lost Universe 3

In the Buddhist temple

Buddha

Welcome, dear strangers. What brings you here?

Divine

We are on a long journey searching for enlightenment. We need to save your universe from the conspiracy of monsters. Furthermore, we have already faced two opponents and won. Nobody has achieved this feat before. We are a space-time traveler, the group of " The Seer" series.

Buddha

Magnificent. You can call me Buddha. I am the master of spiritual sciences. I'm glad you arrived. Furthermore, I am honored with your visit, as I know that I am before the most capable person in the world. What are your names?

Divine

You can call me Divine. But I am also known as a psychic or child of God. These who accompany me are my adventure partners.

Guardian

Exactly. I am the spirit of the mountain. From the beginning, I have accompanied this young man on his adventures. It is a great honor to participate in this saga that has become the most important series in the world. We are here to teach, learn and evolve. I think this is the duty of every living being in this world of atonement and trials.

Renato

My name is Renato. I am the adopted son of the guardian and a great friend of the seer. Together, we are the most important trio in the world. I am delighted with your world. I promise to work hard to protect it.

Buddha

Very well. Make yourselves comfortable. If we are here together, it is because it is written. I never believed in coincidences. But I see now that there is reason and purpose to all things. It's like we're in a movie. We are actors governed by the creator. It is up to each one to play its part.

Guardian

I want some tea. Could you invite us to drink?

Buddha

Of course. We took the opportunity and got to know each other better.

Kitchen

Divine

I still haven't had the courage to ask. But how did this revolution begin?

Buddha

It is written in the book of the apocalypse. First, the plagues started. There was an invasion of locusts, frogs, and snakes. Then they launched a deadly virus in our universe, killing half the inhabitants. Those were difficult times. With that, an alien race took advantage of the situation and invaded our planet. They are terrible monsters that we could not overcome. Thanks to your help, we begin to have hope.

Divine

How nice. We just did our job. There is still a long way to go. We need your positive vibrations. We need to gather courage, strength, and faith like never. But I hope everything will be all right in the end.

Renato

This tea really is wonderful. It makes my mind travel through unknown worlds. I remember everything I have faced so far, there were so many emotions experienced and challenges overcome. But nothing compares to the current moment. We are facing death. But we managed to escape from it twice. Let's take advantage and think about the next steps. Planning is everything.

Guarding

Planning and caring are our motto. Since our series started, we have always had good values that have supported us. Our success it is no coincidence. We are the most prepared to face disasters. With that, we help the creator to coordinate the entire universe.

Buddha

You are the best. Our pride and our hope. What an honor to have you in my home. If you need anything, just talk.

Divine

I need. You said you were a master of spiritual sciences. Can you teach us now?

Buddha

Of course. Follow me on a walk in the forest.

Renato

Finally, everything will start.

Forest

Renato

What is karma?

Buddha

It is the strength of destiny upon us. Good actions produce relevant fruits, while bad actions bind us to materialism. Hence, the concept of "sila", which are our ethical values, which lead us to evolve or regress.

Divine

What is a rebirth?

Buddha

They're our successive reincarnations. Most beings cannot achieve spiritual enlightenment. Therefore, they need to reincarnate several times until they reach complete learning. When that happens, we return to the infinite and loving father. Each reincarnation occurs in one of these six realms: Hell, Animal World, Kingdom of ghosts, World of men, kingdom of gods and paradise.

Guardian

What is " The cycle of Samsara "?

Buddha

These are the cycles of natural existence. There is a concentration of suffering and frustrations. It comprises the upper and lower worlds.

Renato

What are the four noble truths?
Buddha
Life leads us to suffering; Suffering is caused by desire; When the desire is over, the suffering is also over; The path of enlightenment is the path of the Buddha.
Divine
Very interesting. It is always good to know new cultures and visions. Despite this, I have my convictions. We are immaterial beings, created to evolve. We came into the world to learn and teach. The world is a great test and a great mission. We didn't come to judge. We came to hug and help each other. Furthermore, we came to respect each one in their individuality. So, my father loves all good denominations regardless of religion, sexual orientation, political party, race, ethnicity, or gender. We are all children of the same father. I have come to shine, and I am the salvation of all the desperate. I am the defender of the poor, homosexuals and excluded.
Buddha
You have my admiration. You are the master of masters. Someone who is worth listening to. The world needs more people like that.
Guardian
You're right. The son of God is a wonderful person. But we must respect everyone's free will. This is the greatest achievement of all.
Renato
Because we are free, we can think and act freely. Because we are free, we have a chance to be happy.
Buddha
In the end, we all seek the same thing: the reunion with the father. I hope you are lucky in this endeavor and free us from monsters.
Divine
May God hear you.

The Lost Universe 4

Street

Divine

Oh my God! Where were you? It is a pleasure to see you.

Beatriz

The pleasure is mine. Something made me move here.

Divine

I understand. But it's really a coincidence to see each other here after so long. I had already lost my hopes of seeing you again.

Beatriz

I still believed at this moment and believe: There are no coincidences.

Divine

But what is the meaning of this?

Beatriz

We don't know yet, but I'm here to teach and learn. I have been researching, and I am now before a recognized writer. I want to learn a little about your world with you and vice versa. Now, I need your yes to continue.

Divine

Yes.

Guardian

I am also willing.

Renato

It will be a pleasure.

Beatriz

Follow me.

Home Room

Beatriz

I'm a Wicca!

Divine

I do not care. Furthermore, I know the depths of your soul and I know it wouldn't hurt anyone.

Beatriz

Exactly. But I ended up doing harm to myself. This is one of the reasons I came back. I want to stay on top of my lifelong goals with your help. I can only trust you. On the other hand, I will give subsidy for you to meet my world and can then write a wonderful episode.

Divine

It will be a pleasure to help you.

Guardian

I would also like to participate.

Renato

Together, we are stronger.

Beatriz

Thank you all. Let's get everyone together, then.

Beatriz

Well, I'm Wicca. Welcome, everyone. Before introducing you to my world, I will give you a general dimension of how it got started. Having the current dimension given by the English official Gerald Brosseau Gardnet, Wicca is a religiosity that is based on the natural cycles of the land being stratified in rites of passage, initiation, and priesthood. We could more accurately define it as the natural science of man and his relationship with nature. In no way, can it be compared to classical witchcraft and is not contrary to the ideas of any religion? It is a philosophical doctrine that aims to rescue the concept of female and male divinity. Contrary to what they point out, we seek spiritualization, peace with ourselves and the environment. We have control of the magic and the use is individual. Knowing how to carry a weapon is the best form of control.

Renato

What exactly is magic in the Wicca concept?

Beatriz

According to master Phillip Bonevits, magic is a science and an art that comprises a system of concepts and methods for the construction of human emotion. It alters the electrochemical balance of the metabolism, using several techniques and associated instruments to concentrate and focus this emotional energy. In this way, it modulates the energy spread by the human body to affect other energy patterns, animate or inanimate. Although it occasionally affects personal energy patterns.

Guardian

Magic is everything we do that connects us to a higher force. In a classic appearance, we have black magic and white magic. As I understand, the use of it in Wicca depends on the nature of the individual.

Beatriz

As in any other denomination, friend.

Divine

I understand that black magic is to envy, slander, wish evil and do work in spiritual centers to harm your fellow man. White magic is a mental concentration for the good. An example of this are the prayers directed to God.

Renato

The future of wizards and unfair in general is the sea of mud, fire, and brimstone. In the opposite direction, the righteous will shine like stars in the sky.

Divine

With the proviso that salvation is still possible if there is sincere repentance and an effective change of life. I promise that for my father, all his dark past will be forgotten, and the light will shine for you.

Beatriz

It is with this hope that I gather with you. Here is a sinner aware of all the wrong I've done. Give me a chance to give back a little to remedy what I did.

Divine

I give you a chance.

Renato

Me too.

Guardian

With God's permission, yes. You have all my support.

Beatriz

You are wonderful. Count on me for everything.

Renato

Continuing the conversation: Beatriz, what do you think of the religions or sects in which the participants think they are better than others or still think they are the only way to salvation?

Beatriz

I've joined a Wicca group by choice and necessity. I was very curious about spiritual matters and relates to magic. It wasn't how I thought, and I don't know if I would do the same thing today. But for the little that I learned, our group is not like others that only think in numbers of supporters. We respect the options of our fellow man.

Divine

Especially because the paths for my father are multiple. The forces of good are present in all good beliefs that preach peace and harmony between beings. So, one way for you to differentiate between good and evil is to observe its fruits.

Beatriz

Truth. What brought you into this world?

Guardian

This world has been invaded by monsters. We are trying to rescue him.

Beatriz

Interesting. I expected no less from you. You are very competent.

Divine

Thanks, friend. We feel obliged to help. In return, we wrote a beautiful story.

Renato

The future of the "Lost Universe" is in our hands. We have to really live it up.

Beatriz

Very well. Finally, what is your opinion of me, Divine?

Divine

I'm suspicious to talk, but I've always liked you. Since high school, we've been best friends. I know that everyone makes mistakes, but that can be fixed. Therefore, I have hope that you will reflect and find your true path.

Beatriz

I am convinced. You are my way and my light. I'll be rooting for you, Divine. Free this world and make history. You deserve it more than anyone.

Divine

You were smart to change your mind. There is still hope.

The Lost Universe 5

African religion

Black Man

I'm glad you arrived safely. Welcome to the African world.

Divine

Thank you, our new master. We are ready to learn.

Renato

The "lost universe" is very similar to our world. It surprises me.

Guardian

Because he is the reflection of our world. A form of escape from fear itself. A reflection is then necessary.

Black Man

Let's start the conversation immediately.

Renato

What is the concept of God in Umbanda?

Black Man

We believe in a single omnipotent, omniscient and omnipresent God.

Divine

What do you believe about spirits?

Black Man

We believe in superior spirits. We call them Orishas.

Guardian

What do you think about reincarnation?

Black Man

We believe there is.

Renato
How do you see death?
Black man.
We believe in life after death. The spirit lives following its cycle of evolution.
Divine
What is a mediumship?
Black Man
It is the ability to communicate with spirits.
Guardian
What else does Umbanda preach?
Black Man
Man reaps what he sows; Everything that happens in our life is a consequence of free will; Follow the master's advice: love each other and do unto others as you would have them do unto you.
Divine
That's what I always do. I preach respect, equality, and tolerance. We are all children of the same holy father. No one can judge anyone. We all have the right to do what we want with our lives.
Black Man
Exactly, friend. We agree on that.
Divine
Could you talk a little about Candomblé?
Black Man
Of course. It will be a pleasure. Candomblé is a monotheistic religion. We believe in a single creative God. This God created the orishas, nature's spirits. Orishas are spiritual beings with their personality, diverse abilities and unique preferences. We believe in the afterlife and mediumship.
Divine
Very enlightening. Thanks for the information.
Black Man
Well, now, let's change the subject. How do you intend to protect us from monsters?

Guardian

We are putting our plan into practice. We face monsters with intelligence. Furthermore, we allow them to attack. After, we hit them back, with our powerful mind. This favored us four times. I believe it is the recipe for success.

Black Man

Very well. I'm glad you thought about it.

Renato

How do you feel regarding this alien invasion?

Black Man

I have never been so scared in my whole life. It's not what I'm used to. We feel powerless because we cannot react. Thank God you arrived and are changing this situation.

Divine

I am happy to know that our work is bearing fruit. You can always count on us. We are here to protect all the defenseless.

Black Man

Thank you very much. I appreciate the opportunity. Being before the son of God is truly an honor. I would like to know him better. Could you tell us a little about yourself?

Divine

Of course, yes. Can we come into your house?

Black Man

Yes. You are officially invited.

Guardian

Thank you.

Living room

Guardian

The little dreamer entered my life at the top of the mountain. He was a young man with many dreams. The sacred mountain was his only hope of success after years of failed attempts at art. With my help, he undertook challenges and entered the most dangerous cave in the world. He became the seer, an omniscient being, through his visions. Since then, there have been countless dangerous adventures. My testimony is that I am increasingly surprised with this young man.

Renato

The psychic was the man who freed me from my father. After this bad phase, I could live with my master intense emotions. I am proud to be your adventure partner.

Divine

The guardian of the mountain and Renato were the pillars of my rebirth. With their help, I became a real winner. I am a being full of courage, faith, and hope. Despite always remembering my suffering childhood and adolescence, I was reborn at the right time. Today, I am a writer, composer, filmmaker and civil servant. All of this makes up my authorial world. It is a world of delights, where minorities are important. I am a loving, caring and unprejudiced father. I think my destiny is to conquer the world.

Black Man

I'm rooting for you. Don't mind the reviews or enemies. You are bigger than them. Its mission on earth is "to set an example and help people". That's why you're so capable. Your mother must be very proud.

Divine

Thanks for the support. My family is proud of me despite the relationship problems. She is my support in difficult times.

Black Man

I realized that. Your search for the "meaning of life" is a fertile way of learning. Try to focus on the good taste of life, and all these things shall be added unto you.

Divine

Hopefully. I will still be fully happy, but I don't know exactly when. At this time, I won't worry about the future. I need to live day after day and build my story.

Black Man

It will be a beautiful story. I'll be rooting for you and for my world. We need that powerful man within you to save us. We need to remain hopeful in the face of a devastated world.

Divine
You will have hope. I commit myself.
Guardian
Let's up the stakes a little. We will face danger with all our strength. Faith will guide us.
Renato
I just hope it goes well.

The Lost Universe 6

house
spirits
I'm glad you came. The time has come to find out what spiritism is.
Renato
Fantastic! We are very anxious.
Divine
We will be listening carefully.
Guardian
Who is God?
Spirit person
It is the origin of all things and the source of universal love.
Renato
What is the duty of man?
Spirit person
Love God above all things and your neighbor as yourself.
Divine
What is the soul?
Spirit person
It is the spiritual part of the human being that is disembodied from the body at the moment of death.
Guardian
What is death?
Spirit person
Death process. The soul survives and follows its evolutionary path.

Renato

What is reincarnation?

These are the various lives of the spirit on earth, or in other words. It happens when the human being needs to progress. Many of us are part of this natural process.

Divine

What else could you tell us about spiritism?

Spirit person

It is a methodology of life. We believe in the protection and love of the creator at all times. Therefore, it is not necessary to follow specific rules. We need to evolve and the practice of charity is the main one. Without charity, there is no salvation. And you? What do you preach?

Divine

I am the good shepherd. Love God above all things and be good with each other. God is the only one worthy of worship. Do not torment God with your vain concerns. Rather, try to solve the problems. Work and rest; Honor parents and family; Do not kill; Be loyal to your partner; Do not practice sexual perversions like Zoophilia, pedophilia, and incest. Work hard instead of stealing; Don't lie; Don't be jealous; Practice simplicity, honesty, dignity, and loyalty. Be responsible at work. Avoid the game; Do not use any drugs. Never harm the subordinate because the world goes around many times. Be tolerant, accept the different. Do not judge and you will not be judged. Don't think no harm to nobody as the law of return is strict. Do not give in to the devil's temptations. You know, the price is too high. Forgive, but always remember the facts, so you don't hurt yourself again. Once the trust is broken, you never get it back. Do charity and good deeds every day. I assure you: Whoever engages in charity, their sins will be forgiven. Comfort the sick and desperate; There will be plagues, signs in space, earthquakes, volcanic eruptions, tsunamis, wars between kingdoms and loss of faith in Christ. Those who survive are the chosen ones of the kingdom. Therefore, prayer is your primary weapon against calamity. You are a house built on rock that the wind and the storm can't bring down. For those who continue to fight for your happiness and success, I have a message: I am with you. I am the little hope that remains in you. Behold, I tell you that this little flame can lead you to victory. I am the way, the truth, and the life. I will have mercy on those who have mercy, and I will give love to those who have given me love. You are free to choose your path. I gave you free will for my love. I know that there are significant disagreements and wickedness in the world. But it was my best decision when creating humanity. Remember that everyone is my child. I created good and evil, necessary forces for the balance of the world. But I am the only God, omnipotent, omniscient and omnipresent. As long as there is a world, it will be this way. You want to avoid being like me, some great misfortune will befall you if you do. Pray a lot for you and for the world. I will never leave you nor forsake you.

Guardian

We just heard a pronouncement from Christ.

Divine

Truth. He's always with me. We are interconnected.

Renato

Amazing. It is very exciting to receive that message. It is an honor and a joy to be in the presence of Christ.

Spirit person

I am thrilled. It was a gorgeous blessing. The world needs good news. The worldwide pandemic has shown us how fragile we are. This is a signal to the world. We need to learn from it and become better people. We also need divine help to drive out the monsters. My people need peace and hope.

Guardian

Exactly, friend. Don't worry about anything. That leaves it in our laps. It is a great challenge and exercise for our group. The knowledge of religions, the connection between worlds and dangerous monsters makes this story the most important so far. Take it easy.

Spirit person

I can't be calm. My people are being wiped out by these aliens. They are highly cruel and powerful beings. I fear for your life.

Renato

Do not worry. Powerful angels accompany us. Nothing bad is going to happen.

Divine

We are protected and strategists. Your world is in good hands. We know that it is a great challenge, but this can be overcome. In fact, nothing is impossible for us. The impossible is within our reach. Our limit is only the limit of the imagination. Good episodes will be written in our history. I'm sure one of them is this one.

Spirit person

You are quite optimistic. That's perfect. I admire you for your effort. Continue the journey. I will be rooting for our victory.

Renato

So be it.

The Lost Universe 7

forest

Guardian

We are on a long journey. It is the right time to reflect, position ourselves and plan. This world and its people are languishing. We therefore need to act promptly.

Renato

I believe that we are on the right path. There is much to question, but we have made progress. We have overcome many adversities, and we are still in control. We are big winners.

Divine

I agree with both. I'm reflecting a lot. This reminds me of my trajectory. I see my childhood suffered in the interior of the northeast, experiencing financial difficulties. I fought against misery, indifference, and prejudice. No matter how hard I tried, my dreams became more and more difficult. I gave up and resumed my artistic activities several times. Something bigger sustained me. A compelling force of hope. I had to try. Little by little, I was advancing in my projects. I got a job, and it gave me greater motivation. Hope has reappeared. Currently, I continue to fight. I'm moving on. The advice I give does that everyone follow this example. We must not give up on our dreams.

Renato

Exactly. How do you analyze the previous adventures?

Divine

Opposing forces was the kickoff. At the time, I was just an immature young man with an artist's dream. I always dreamed of sharing my stories with the public. It was just a dream that became viable by climbing the mountain. That's when I met you. Together, we overcame challenges and traveled through time. We arrived in Mimoso, a place dominated by political authoritarianism, by a bad witch and by great inequality. My great task was " to balance the forces of dark and light " and help someone find their way. For thirty days, I experienced intense emotions. In the second adventure, I could explore capital sins. On a trip to a desert island, I could find new challenges and understand "My dark night of the soul", a dark period in my history where I sank into sins. I went, saw and won. In the third stage, I went back to the past in the "Brazilian Northeast". I could find my origins and understand pertinent questions. In the fourth challenge, I discovered "god's secret code", something never achieved before. Afterwards, I traveled through space, gained new knowledge and here I am. Everything I learned served to my evolutionary process. I do not regret anything.

Renato

I feel pleased because I am able to give this testimony. It is a great pleasure to participate in this series, which has become the most important in the world.

Divine

Thank you, friend. Any guidance, guardian of the mountain?

Guardian

We are approaching the next goal. I recommend caution and precaution. The enemy can be anywhere.

Divine

Okay. Let's move on.

Temple

Guardian

The Jews and Romans killed Jesus.

Divine

The messiah has already come, and they did not recognize it. They expected a leader who could free them from Roman slavery. But they wanted to avoid recognizing Jesus, the moral leader. Someone who died for our sins.

Renato

Why has it come to this? Fortunately, Christ was resurrected and became the main leader on the planet. This shows that his doctrine is true because his project comes from God.

Guardian

We all have freedom of choice. Each one must be respected. Jesus made history. He is the God of the lowly and marginalized. The God of prostitutes, poor and tax collectors. Anyway, he is the God of all the marginalized.

Jesus

Thankfully, you speak well of me.

Guardian

Is you Jesus?

Jesus

I am the lion of David. I came to give my moral support to your project. Furthermore, I admire your willingness to fight dangerous monsters. I am enjoying learning about religions. Truly, I am in all good religions. The important thing is to do good.

Renato

What will we do in difficult times?

Jesus

Even though I walk through the darkest valley, I will fear no evil, for you, are with me; your rod and your staff, they comfort me.

Guardian

Why, occasionally, we did not achieve all the goals?

Jesus

Because you have so little faith. Truly I tell you, if you have faith as small as a mustard seed, you can say to this mountain, move from here to there, and it will move. Nothing will be impossible for you.

Truly I tell you, if you have faith and do not doubt, not only can you do what was done to the fig tree, but also you can say to this mountain, Go, throw yourself into the sea, and it will be done.

Divine

What awaits us in the future?

Jesus

Behold, the day of the LORD comes, cruel, with wrath and fierce anger, to make the land a desolation and to destroy its sinners from it.

Jesus

There will be signs in the sun, moon and stars. On the earth, nations will be in anguish and perplexity at the roaring and tossing of the sea.

People will faint from terror, apprehensive of what is coming to the world, for the heavenly bodies will be shaken.

Jesus

But the day of the Lord will come like a thief. The heavens will disappear with a roar; the elements will be destroyed by fire, and the earth and everything done in it will be laid bare.

Divine

The good thing is to be prepared for the end. Do we have a chance to save this universe?

Jesus

Believe me. I will guide you. Peace and good for all.

Final forest

Guardian

The end has come. We are free.

Renato

Hallelujah. I appreciate these incredible moments. It was really wonderful.

Guardian

What message do you give us, dear son of God?

Divine

I have a message for this universe. In this time of crisis, where we had plagues, divine signs and extra-terrestrial invasion, we can reflect on how small we are. The entire universe is from God. We are just their little creatures. By recognizing our humility, we can finally evolve. All is fleeting but the power of God remains. Learn the true value of things. This world has survived, and we have survived by faith in God. The world will remain because of the good. Until the next adventure.

The End

www.ingramcontent.com/pod-product-compliance
Lightning Source LLC
LaVergne TN
LVHW021050100526
838202LV00082B/5426